Slumberkins®

This book belongs to

Scan here for additional Slumberkins resources and content.

The Costume Comeback at the Monster Ball

By Kelly Oriard with Callie Christensen

Illustrated by Noona Vinogradoff

The moon hung bright in the sky
one harvest night in fall.
An exciting event was coming,
everyone's favorite:

The Monster Ball!

Sloth was one of many kins
to dress up and paint his face.
His mom made a special costume
that came straight from outer space.

1.

Light green from his antennae
to the tip of every toe,
Sloth hoped his stellar costume
would help him steal the show!

3.

"I want to be like Unicorn
and stand out in the crowd!"
Sloth danced around excitedly
as he wished his wish out loud.

4.

5.

Walking to the Monster Ball,
    he stopped and looked around.
Spiders, bats, and even ghosts
    were everywhere to be found.

"We must be getting close!"
    He was ready for the ball.
But then he felt his feelings change
    with each new kin he saw.

6.

Alpaca's suit of pumpkin orange
glimmered a brilliant sheen,

and Dragon made the best peacock
that Sloth had ever seen!

He noticed all the costumes
    and wondered, "Should I have come?"
Comparing himself to other kins
    really wasn't very fun.

So bright! So bold! So colorful!
   Everything Sloth wished to be.
His body went from hot to cold–
   "I wish that could be me!

"I want to change my costume now.
   This one's not right at all!
I can't wear this!" he cried aloud,
   as his mom walked him to the ball.

9.

"It's too late to change your costume,"
said his mom with a kind voice.
"Sometimes we have to stick with things
once we've made a choice.

"Your costume may be unique,
but that's just part of the fun!
You can be proud to be yourself
and stand out from everyone."

11.

12.

Sloth groaned and grumbled;
  then agreed with a sigh
and turned to his mom
  to hug her goodbye.

He paused for a moment
  outside of the door.
Could he be strong and brave
  about the costume he wore?

13.

15.

The Monster Ball was quite a sight.
It was full of exciting things!
Sloth then noticed that even Frank
wore a shade of ghoulish green!

16.

As he thought about his feelings,
Ghost Floof fluttered by.
Dragon followed behind, but stopped–
Sloth had caught their eye!

"What's wrong, my friend?" said Dragon.
"You look like you feel down."
"My costume is too boring,"
Sloth answered with a frown.

18.

"But your costume is so creative.
   It looks like it could glow!"
Dragon grinned, "In just a bit,
   you'll surely steal the show."

Sloth felt so confused.
   Just what had Dragon meant?
Then Vlad and Frank surprised them all
   with a new harvest-time event.

"It's time to dance the...

NiGHT LiGHT DANCE!"

Vlad called out with a shout.
Then as Frank turned the music on,
the party's lights went out!

All around the dance floor
costumes glowed with a soft light.
And Sloth's own cosmic costume
was the brightest of the night!

22.

23.

As Sloth danced with his friends,
   he realized something new.
Sometimes it works out best,
   when you see your choices through.

"I feel so bold and bright tonight!
   I'm so happy I stuck it out.
It can be a tricky feeling
   when you suddenly have self-doubt."

24.

Unicorn took Sloth's hand
   and said, "This is just so great.
We're both similar yet different–
   there is much to celebrate."

Sloth started feeling better,
   as the Monster Ball went on.
He liked dancing with his friends,
   and all his shame was gone.

Pumpkin Carving

We sometimes change our minds about
the things we say or do.
But good things can also happen
when we see our choices through!

27.

I can make strong decisions
and be proud to stand out.
Embracing my feelings,
is what bravery is all about.

28.

Reflect & Connect

Worries and fears of being accepted and belonging can create a lot of turmoil for children. This can lead to pushing their own feelings down and changing who they are to fit in. This story can reassure children that they are enough just as they are and remind them they can stand out and be proud of their true selves.

———— Deepen the Learning ————

(1) Has there ever been a time when you made a choice that you later wished you could have changed?

(2) Have you ever wished you could change a situation, but then everything worked out in the end?

(3) Sloth started to compare himself to others on his way to the Monster Ball. Have you ever compared yourself to others? What did it feel like to do that?

Adult Engagement: Can you remember a time when you have been unsure about a choice you made and how you handled it? Were you able to stand up for yourself and be proud?

slumberkins

Discover a World of Feelings

From understanding emotions to strengthening their inner voice, give children the

The Caring Crew

IBEX — EMOTIONAL COURAGE · YETI — MINDFULNESS · SLOTH — ROUTINES · OTTER — BUILDING CONNECTIONS · HONEY BEAR — GRATITUDE

The Confidence Crew

BIGFOOT — SELF-ESTEEM · UNICORN — AUTHENTICITY · HAMMERHEAD — CONFLICT RESOLUTION · NARWHAL — GROWTH MINDSET · YAK — SELF-ACCEPTANCE

The Resilience Crew

FOX — CHANGE · ALPACA — STRESS RELIEF · SPRITE — GRIEF AND LOSS · LYNX — SELF-EXPRESSION · DRAGON — CREATIVITY

30.